FACTORY FRESH!

Based on the teleplay by Kyle McCulloch • Illustrated by Harry Moore

A GOLDEN BOOK • NEW YORK

created by

Stephen Hillenburg

randomhousekids.com
ISBN 978-1-5247-1430-7
Printed in the United States of America
10 9 8 7 6 5 4 3 2 1

SpongeBob and Patrick were spending a perfect day together. They jellyfished. They brushed each other's teeth. They even wore the same pants. SpongeBob knew there was only one way to end the day.

"Buying ourselves the perfect ice cream! What kind should we get? HØGAN DÜP?" he asked.

"That's too fancy," Patrick replied.

"Rocky road!" they yelled together.

"With real rocks," Patrick added.

"Unlike our friendship, which is a smooth avenue, and will never have any bumps," SpongeBob said.

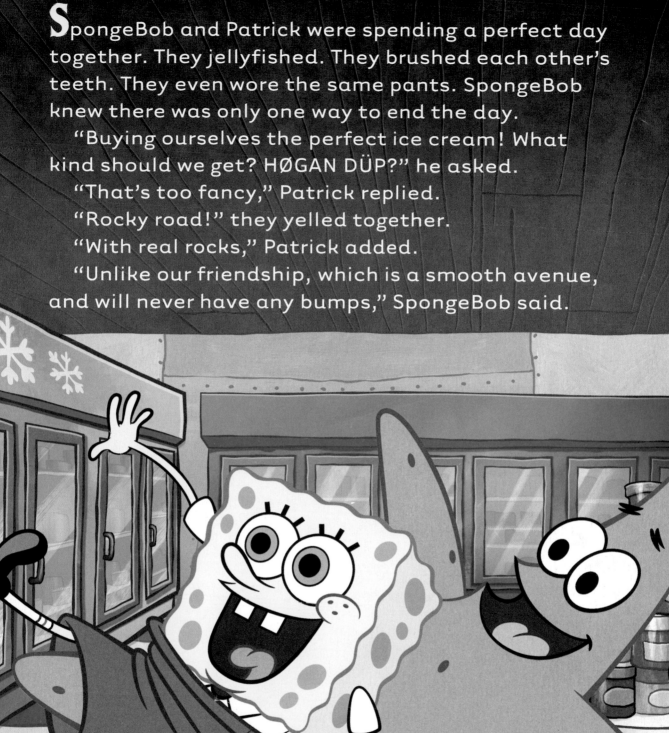

At the supermarket, SpongeBob and Patrick ran into Mr. Krabs buying a Lonely Krab Dinner for One.

"I can't believe what they're charging for this frozen debris!" he said.

"Can you imagine if they had frozen Krabby Patties at the supermarket?" SpongeBob said.

Mr. Krabs's eyes lit up. "That's a million-dollar idea I just had that you said before me."

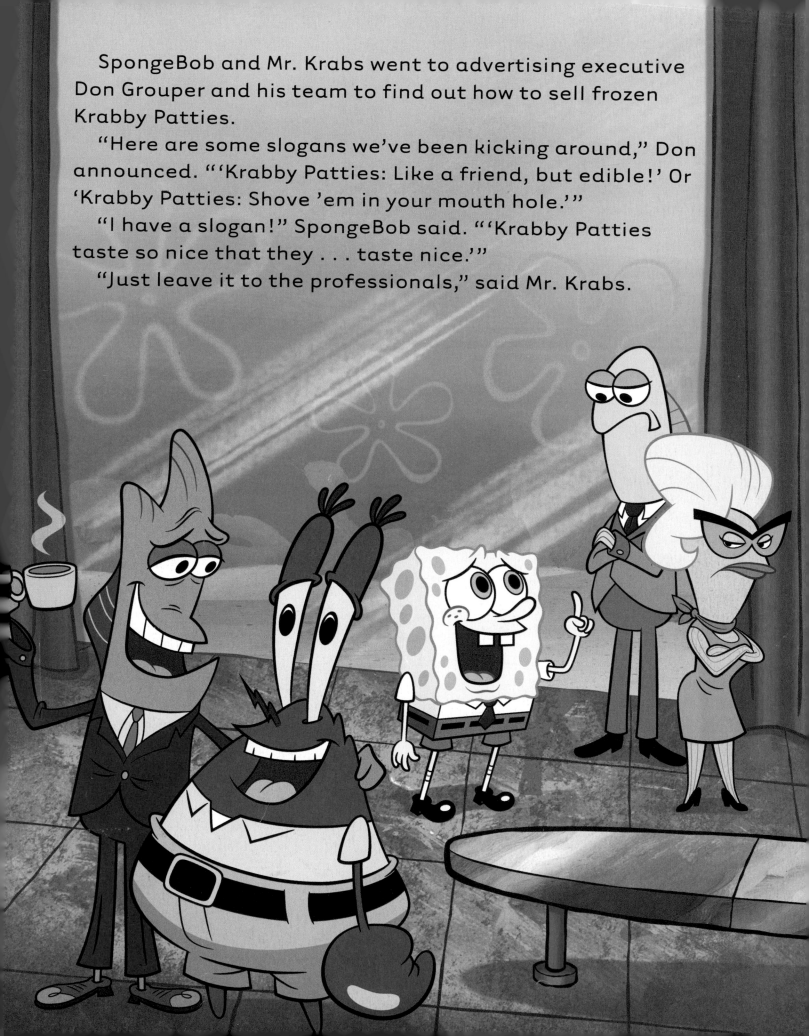

SpongeBob and Mr. Krabs went to advertising executive Don Grouper and his team to find out how to sell frozen Krabby Patties.

"Here are some slogans we've been kicking around," Don announced. "'Krabby Patties: Like a friend, but edible!' Or 'Krabby Patties: Shove 'em in your mouth hole.'"

"I have a slogan!" SpongeBob said. "'Krabby Patties taste so nice that they . . . taste nice.'"

"Just leave it to the professionals," said Mr. Krabs.

Don needed a star for the commercial. "We want a regular guy to represent all consumers. A face that says 'I love Krabby Patties.'"

"I've got the perfect guy for the job," Mr. Krabs said. SpongeBob was certain they'd choose him.

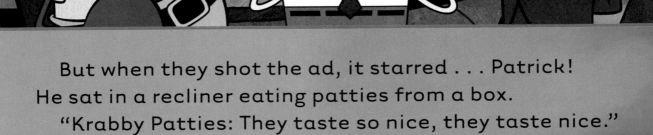

But when they shot the ad, it starred . . . Patrick! He sat in a recliner eating patties from a box.

"Krabby Patties: They taste so nice, they taste nice."

Before Mr. Krabs and SpongeBob left, Don said, "We ran some numbers and realized you could make a lot more money if you change the formula."

"Let's fill 'er up with filler!" Mr. Krabs exclaimed.

SpongeBob couldn't believe his boss would change the secret formula. He wondered if things could get any worse.

The next morning, things got worse. While the frozen Krabby Patties were being made in a factory, Mr. Krabs turned the Krusty Krab into a museum. Then he fired SpongeBob from the restaurant and hired him to give tours and work in the gift shop.

"But what if someone wants a Krabby Patty?" SpongeBob asked.

"We've got plenty in the freezer," Mr. Krabs replied. "Customers at the museum can cook the Krabby Patties themselves."

"What about me?" Squidward asked, walking in from the kitchen.

"Don't worry, Squidward," Mr. Krabs said. "You're fired."

"Will I get hired for a new job at the museum, too?"

"No. You're just fired."

Squidward was overjoyed. "I am free to follow my dreams of being a ballet dancer!"

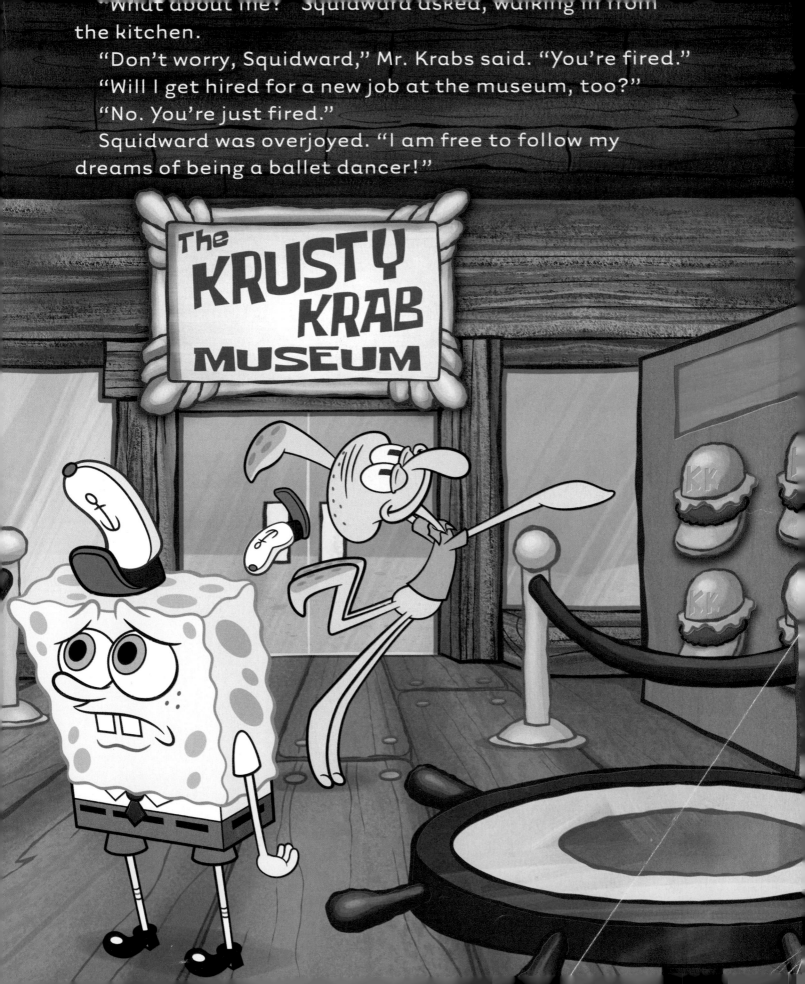

In the weeks that followed, Mr. Krabs sold loads of frozen Krabby Patties and made lots of money.
Patrick became a big star and signed many autographs.

But SpongeBob wasn't happy. He had nothing to do as fewer and fewer people visited the museum. He sensed something was wrong.

One night, SpongeBob went to Patrick's cool new apartment to celebrate his friend's four hundredth commercial. He'd brought their favorite ice cream, rocky road.

But SpongeBob couldn't get near Patrick. His old friend was surrounded by fans and photographers.

And when SpongeBob went to put the melting rocky road in Patrick's freezer, he found it stocked with—fancy ice cream!

Had he lost his friend forever?

Times were so bleak that Squidward returned to the Krusty Krab and begged for a job.

SpongeBob said he could help with the animatronic Squidward. "There's something about him that seems a little off."

"I love my job!" the robotic prop said. "Thanks for coming!"

Squidward kicked it out of the way and took its place. "I hate everyone," he announced in a robot voice. "Ahh, much better."

SpongeBob missed his old job and his best friend. "These frozen Krabby Patties have ruined my life, and it was all my idea," he moaned. "Who I am to fight the future?" He took a bite of a patty and grimaced. "It tastes like sand—and not good sand!"

"What do you think Krabs uses as filler?" Squidward asked.

"Krabby Patties aren't made with sand—they're made with love!" SpongeBob exclaimed.

And that gave him an idea.

SpongeBob reached into his head and found the real, original Krabby Patty recipe. He grabbed his trusty spatula and went to work.

SpongeBob cooked through the night. When he was
done, he had created something wonderful.
"Freshly grilled Krabby Patty, you and I are going to
save the world—and a friendship!" he proclaimed

The next morning, Patrick looked down from his penthouse and saw SpongeBob. It had been a long time since they'd hung out. Patrick ran after him.

"I missed you," SpongeBob said.

"I missed you, too," Patrick said.

"I've got something for you, from one friend to another," SpongeBob said, holding out the still-sizzling patty.

Patrick didn't think he could eat another patty—but this one was different. He took a bite. "It's as delicious as our friendship!" he exclaimed.

"Now that we've saved our friendship, we have to save the reputation of the Krabby Patty!" said SpongeBob.

Patrick would be addressing the shareholders that night at a gala dinner and the premiere of the four hundredth commercial. He knew he had to do something.

At the gala, Don Grouper introduced Patrick. The crowd cheered as he approached the podium. But Patrick couldn't say nice things about the frozen Krabby Patties. He needed to listen to his heart . . . and his stomach.

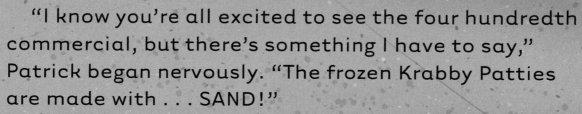

"I know you're all excited to see the four hundredth commercial, but there's something I have to say," Patrick began nervously. "The frozen Krabby Patties are made with . . . SAND!"

People gasped. They opened their mouths and spit out long streams of sand. Don Grouper stormed out of the room. SpongeBob cheered for his friend.

After the big revelation, Mr. Krabs walked sadly through Bikini Bottom. News of the sand had spread across the town.

"It's all gone," he whispered. "Everything I spent my life building is all gone. I'm ruined."

Then he heard a commotion coming from the Krusty Krab Museum.

The Krusty Krab wasn't a museum anymore! All the props had been moved to make room for tables . . . and customers, who were happily eating!

"SpongeBob, did you do all this?" Mr. Krabs asked.

"Absolutely!" The fry cook beamed. "Patrick helped."

"A friend always helps," Patrick said. "It's called *frelping,* and I was very *frelpful.*"

Mr. Krabs was amazed. "But how did you get these customers to eat Krabby Patties? They know they're filled with sand."

"The frozen ones are," SpongeBob said, holding up a juicy patty. "But these are made fresh!"

Mr. Krabs tasted one of SpongeBob's fresh patties. "Oooh! The flavor! The sweet, greasy nectar of the gods! SpongeBob, me boy, you've done a good thing here, lad, but you could use a little *frelp*. How about we partner up and I become your boss and pay you minimum wage while I work you mercilessly?"

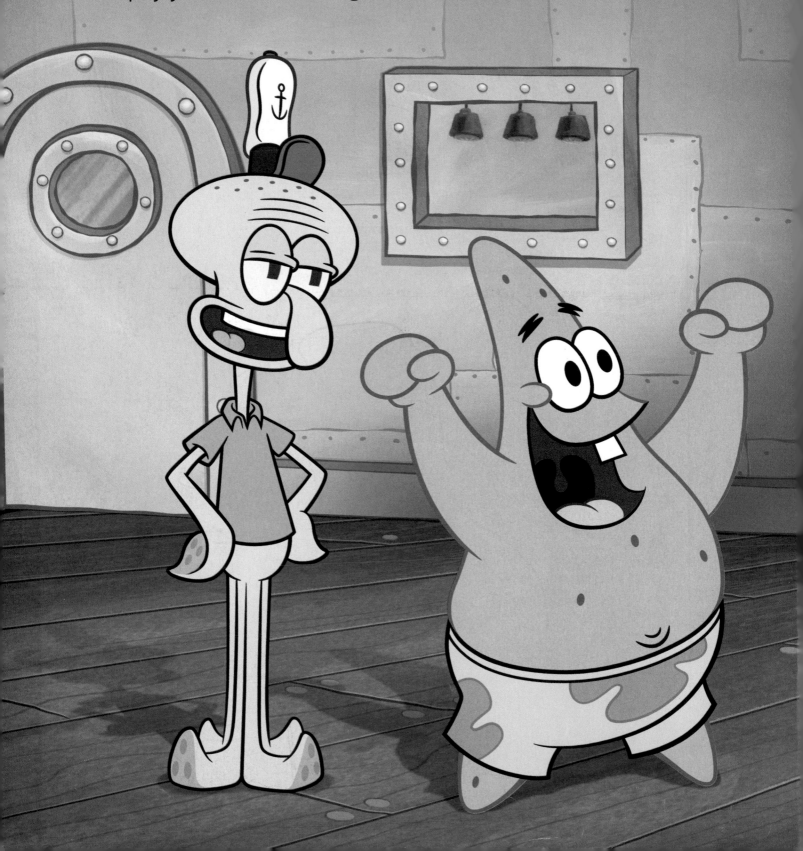

SpongeBob couldn't hide his joy. "Yay! The Krusty Krab is back in business!"

E SPONG FLT
SpongeBob SquarePants :factory fresh!
/

03/17